SPONGEBOB SQUAREPANTS

SPONGEBOB ROCKS!

by Kelli Chipponeri
illustrated by Heather Martinez

SCHOLASTIC INC.

New York Toronto London Auckland Sydney
Mexico City New Delhi Hong Kong Buenos Aires

SpongeBob, Patrick, and Sandy
started a rock band.
They were called Tidal Wave.

Sandy played the guitar.
Patrick played the drums.
SpongeBob was the lead singer.
Their songs "Seaweed Sway,"
"Motion in the Ocean," and
"Jumping Jellyfish" were big hits!

Tidal Wave was the talk of the ocean.
The band had been performing
all over Bikini Bottom.

"Our fans are cooler
than an ice cube in winter!"
Sandy said.

The band was chased by excited fans
from one end of the sea to the other.

At the Krusty Krab . . .

and even on their tour bus!

"We've got to get ready
for our big concert
at the Poseidome!" said SpongeBob.

Tidal Wave practiced for weeks.
"*Jumping, jumping jellyfiiiiiiiiish!*"
SpongeBob sang.

Everyone loved Tidal Wave.
That is, everyone except . . .
Squidward!

"Those fools are just making noise, not music! And they didn't even invite me to play!" Squidward said, grumbling.

That night Squidward
sneaked into SpongeBob's house.

He stole all of the band's
instruments.

The next day, the band
was shocked to find
their instruments missing.

"Who would do this?"
   asked SpongeBob.
"How will we play tonight?"
   asked Sandy.
"What's for lunch?"
   asked Patrick.

SpongeBob, Patrick, and Sandy
sat and thought.
Patrick picked up his drumsticks
and started to tap.
TAP! TAP! TAP-TAP!
"I can't think with you tapping,"
said Sandy.

"Sorry," said Patrick.

"Wait, don't stop," SpongeBob said.

He started tapping on the table.

TAP-TAP! TAP-TAP!

"I have an idea," he said.

19

The band posted flyers
all over Bikini Bottom
asking for the safe return of their
instruments.

Later Tidal Wave arrived
at the famous Poseidome
for their big concert.
"Hey, dudes, where are your drums
and your guitar?"
asked Scooter, a devoted fan.

"We are playing with these tonight,"
said SpongeBob.
He pointed to a sand dollar
and several shells.
"We will be performing 'unplugged,'"
said Sandy.

"What does that mean?"
  asked another fan.
"Patrick will tap on these shells,"
  Sandy explained.
"I will shake the sand dollar,
  and SpongeBob will blow into this
  big conch shell."

SpongeBob held the shell up to his mouth and blew. *BRHOOONKKK!* "Cool!" cheered their fans.

Just then Squidward showed up
holding one of the flyers
the band had made.
"I know where your instruments are,"
Squidward said.

"You do? Where are they?"
   asked Sandy.
"I have them," said Squidward,
   a little ashamed.
"I took them from you because
   you did not ask me to be
   in the band."

"We did not know you wanted to be
in the band, Squidward,"
said SpongeBob.
"We would be happy
if you played with us."
"Really?" asked Squidward.
"I brought my clarinet."

"Well, then, I have an idea,"
Sandy said.

Later that night Tidal Wave
took the stage.
Patrick drummed on the shells.
SpongeBob blew on his conch shell.
Sandy shook the sand dollar.

And the newest band member—
Squidward—played his clarinet!
Fans cheered as Tidal Wave
rocked the Poseidome
till the wee hours!

At the end of the concert, everyone yelled, "More!" SpongeBob waved to the fans. "Bikini Bottom rocks!" he yelled.